Birmingham
City Council

Loans are up to 28 days. Fines are charged if items
are not returned by the due date. Items can be renewed
at the Library, via the internet or by telephone up to
3 times. Items in demand will not be renewed.

Please use a bookmark.

www.birmingham.gov.uk/libcat
www.birmingham.gov.uk/libraries

C2 000 005 177734

Eco Activities
PLASTIC

Written by
Louise Nelson

BookLife PUBLISHING

©2022
**BookLife Publishing Ltd.
King's Lynn
Norfolk, PE30 4LS, UK**

All rights reserved.
Printed in Poland.

A catalogue record for this book is available from the British Library.

ISBN: 978-1-83927-266-0

Written by:
Louise Nelson

Edited by:
Robin Twiddy

Designed by:
Jasmine Pointer

CONTENTS

Words that look like <u>this</u> can be found in the glossary on page 24.

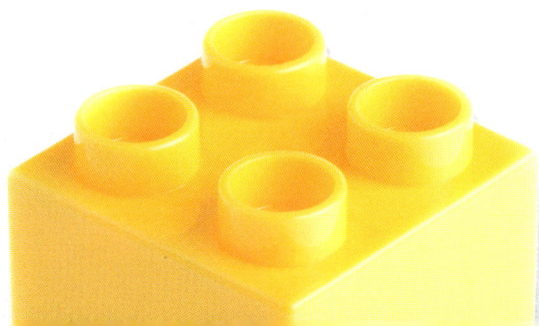

A PLASTIC PLAN

STOP! Don't throw that plastic bottle in the bin! That is really bad for the world, and there are lots of things you could do with it instead.

Did you know?
Many of the things we throw away can be used again for something else.

Every minute, a whole truck's-worth of plastic is thrown into the ocean. We have to stop, but what can we do?

Reduce: Try not to buy plastic.

Reuse: Use your plastic for something new.

Recycle: Make sure you recycle plastic things.

WHAT IS PLASTIC?

Plastic is a material. We use materials, such as wood, glass, paper and metal to make things. Materials have properties. Properties tell us what the material is like.

The Properties of Plastic

Can be shaped into almost any shape

Can be thin and <u>transparent</u> (such as a plastic bag)

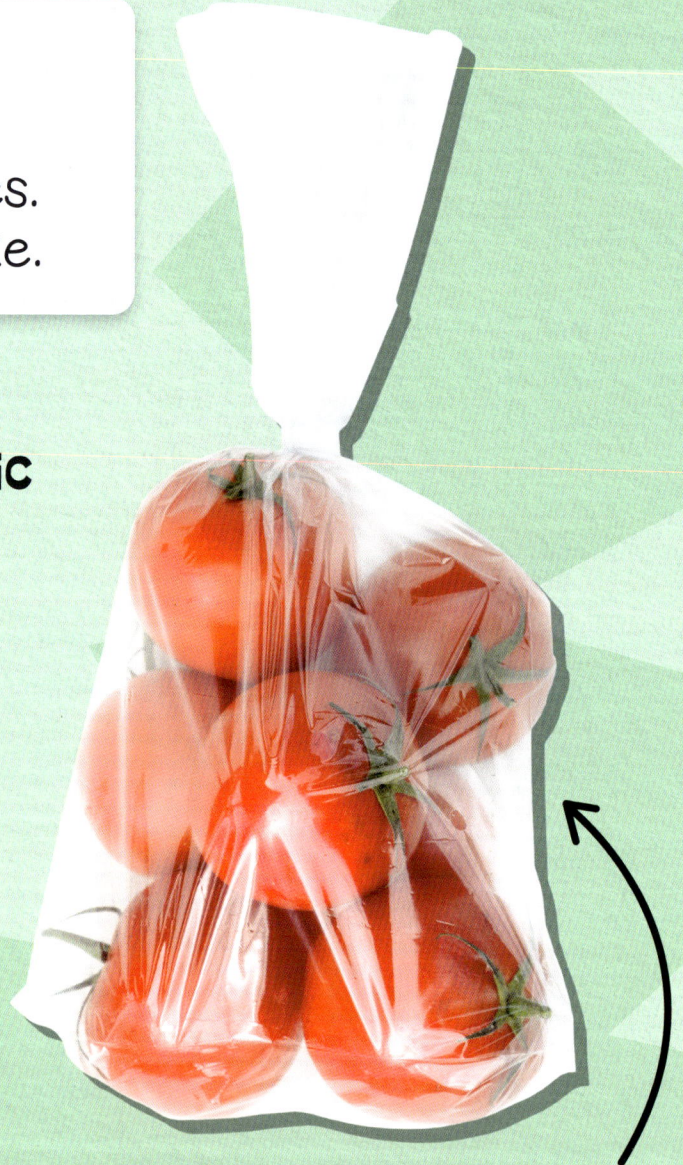

Can be thick and <u>opaque</u> (such as a lunchbox)

Made by people

Can last a long time — even hundreds of years!

A PLASTIC PARADISE

Let's keep that plastic out of the ocean — we can use it to make an ocean scene instead!

This works great as a class project — can you fill a whole wall?

You will need:

- Lots of bottle tops in different colours
- Large piece of cardboard (an old cardboard box will work great)
- Plastic bottles in different colours
- String
- Googly eyes
- Paper and glue
- Marker pens
- Pipe cleaners
- Scissors
- Tape

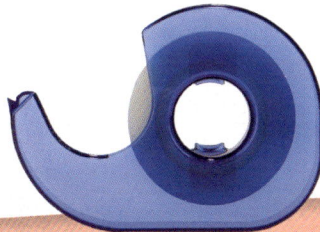

! Safety first! Always ask a grown-up for help. Plastic bottles and scissors can be sharp!

STEP 1. Use the pens to draw your ocean scene.

STEP 2. Colour in your ocean scene.

STEP 3. Use the glue to stick the bottle tops to the picture, following the colours in your drawing. You will create an amazing mosaic effect!

Cut your coloured plastic bottles to make fish.

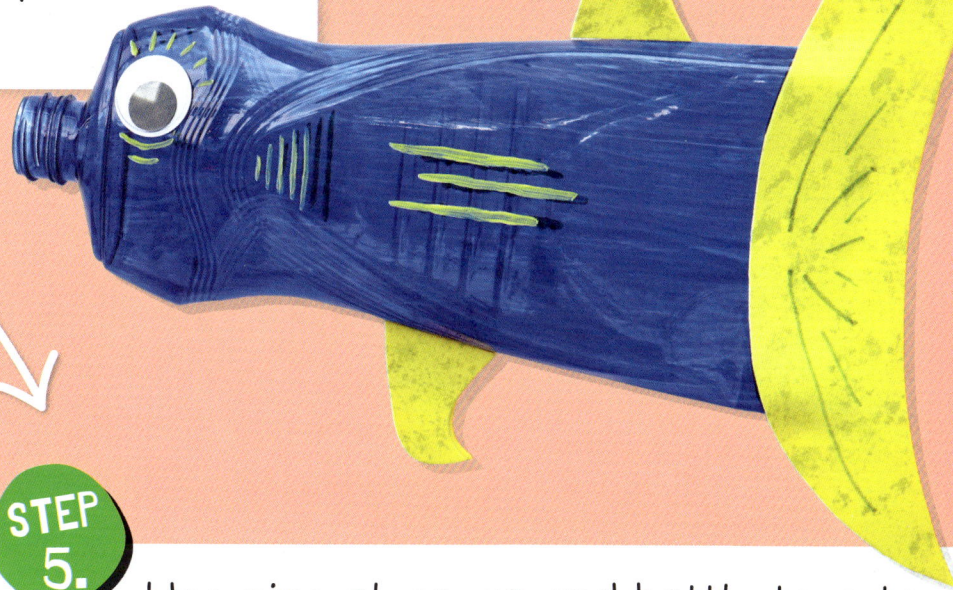

Use pipe cleaners and bottle tops to make other sea creatures, like this crab! What other sea creatures can you make?

Hang your creatures in front of your colourful ocean scene.

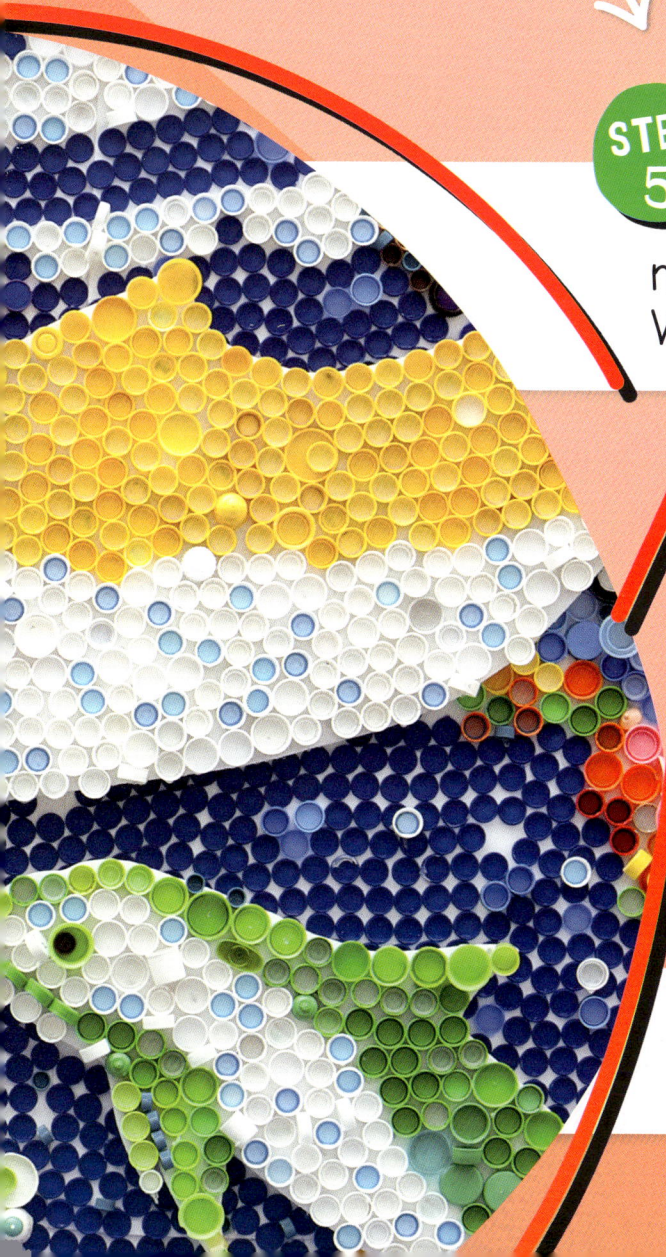

A PLASTIC POSY

Make this lovely bunch of blooms for someone special – or to brighten up a windowsill or garden!

If you want to recycle your flowers afterwards, don't paint them. Use coloured bottles instead.

You will need:

- Plastic drinks bottles (the kind with the bumps at the bottom)
- Acrylic paint
- Paintbrushes
- Thin wooden sticks (to use as stems)
- Felt or paper (for the leaves)
- Paper tape
- Aprons and newspaper
- Scissors

Clean as You Go

Don't forget to put newspaper down in your working area and wear an apron.

13

Ask your grown-up to cut around the knobbly edges of the bottom of the bottle, following the shape made by the bumps.

If you want to, paint inside each bump to look like colourful petals.

14

Glue the flower to a stick.

Glue on the leaves made from felt or paper.

Display your flowers in the garden, in a vase, or tied with a ribbon!

Don't forget — either recycle the rest of the bottle or use it for another project. The top halves of bottles make great greenhouses for seedlings!

PLASTIC POWER!

Plastic rubbish that isn't reused or recycled can end up in the sea. Plastic bags can look like food to hungry turtles, and other rubbish can float around in the water for a long time, <u>polluting</u> our oceans.

When we throw away plastic, it is important to make sure that we do it in the right way.

There are some simple steps to take that can help! When you are done with a plastic item, wash it carefully. Check the label to see which parts of the item can be recycled. Put each part in the right bin.

PLASTIC PLANTERS

These adorable kitty planters will brighten up any windowsill!
Plastic is a good material for plant pots because it is <u>waterproof</u>.

Plastics in the sea can break down into tiny bits called microplastics. Microplastics are small enough to get into the bodies of birds and fish.

You will need:

- Plastic bottles
- Acrylic paint
- Beads, stickers and gems
- Permanent markers
- Stones
- A plant in a pot
- Water

STEP 1. Use the permanent marker to draw around the bottle, remembering to mark on two triangles for cat ears.

STEP 2. Get your grown-up to cut along the lines.

STEP 3. Paint the bottles white.

STEP 4. Use the pens to draw on a kitty face.

STEP 5. Decorate your planter with beads, gems or stickers.

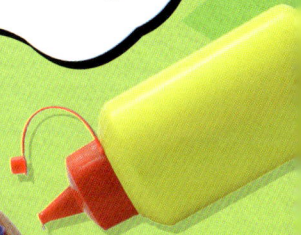

STEP 6. Put a handful of stones into the bottom of the pot to add weight.

STEP 7. Put your plant (in its pot) into the planter.

Don't forget to give your plant a little drink of water too!

PLASTIC PLAY!

These games are simple to make with paper, crayons and bottle tops.

Bottle Top Bingo!

Draw circles on a piece of paper. Colour them in different colours like this. Put different coloured bottle tops into a bag. Now, take it in turns to pick out a bottle top. If it matches a circle on your paper, place it down. The first one to fill their piece of paper wins.

Noughts and Crosses

Turn bottle tops into counters and make travel noughts and crosses too!

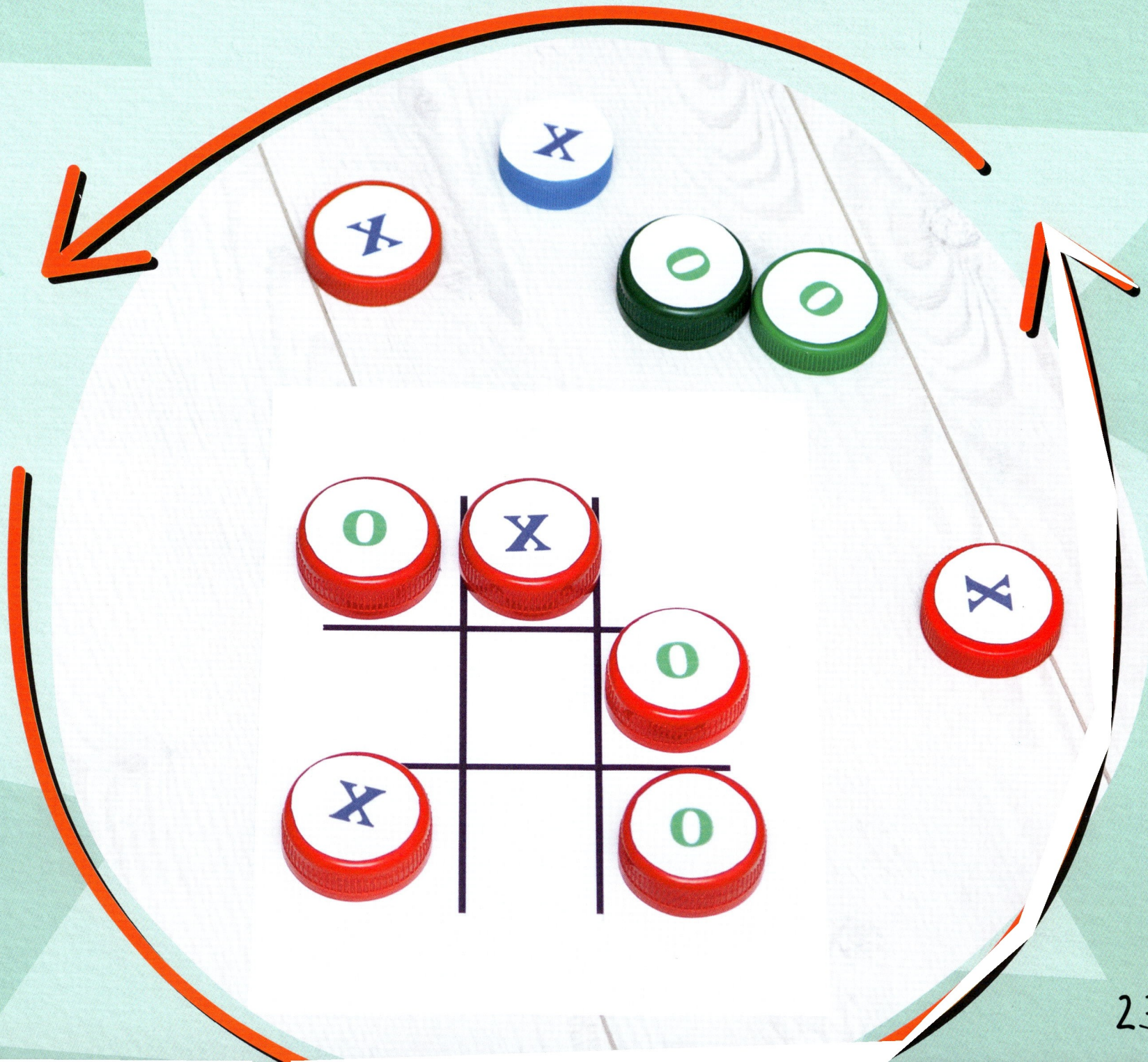

GLOSSARY

greenhouses	glass buildings that are used to grow plants in
mosaic	pictures or patterns that are created by putting together small pieces of stone, tile or glass
opaque	can't be seen through
polluting	when something harmful or poisonous is added to the natural world
recycle	use again to make something else
seedlings	young plants
transparent	can be seen through
waterproof	stops water from getting through

INDEX

PHOTO CREDITS *All images are courtesy of Shutterstock.com, unless otherwise specified. With thanks to Getty Images, Thinkstock Photo and iStockphoto.*
Paper Texture Throughout – Borja Andreu. Front Cover – chuchiko17, 826A IA, KittyVector, elenabsl, Alrandir, sundora14, AlenKadr. 4 – TinnaPong. 5 – Vytas999, Phovoir, Marlon Trottmann, Nastelbo. 6–7 – Janis Smits, MvanCaspel, HeinzTeh, mkos83, Alba_alioth. 8–9 – ESB Professional, Yury Kosourov, Dmitry Kolmakov, IB Photography, Stock Up, Elena Polovinko, SweetLemons, Marija Stepanovic, riphoto3, monticello, Dan Kosmayer, Anton Starikov. 10–11 – peart,ABB Photo, Lee Yiu Tung, Africa Studio, Bushidoh. 12–13 – Wutthichai Phosri, pikselstock, Liliya Krasnova, Becky Starsmore, andregric, BorisShevchuk, Ayrat Gabdrakhmanov, SmileStudio. 14–15 –Wutthichai Phosri, Porstocker. 16–17 – Pixel-Shot, Papakah. 18–19 – chuchiko17, BW Folsom, AlexussK, kak2s, nikkytok. 20–21 – chuchiko17, elenabsl. 22–23 –Vitaliya.